Not Until Christmas, Walter!

POST OFFICE
COFFEE CUP CAFÉ

Not Until Christmas, Walter!

Eileen Christelow

Clarion Books • New York

For Ophelia, with fond memories
of walks through the woods

Winter, 1984 – Fall, 1996

Clarion Books
a Houghton Mifflin Company imprint
215 Park Avenue South, New York, NY 10003

The illustrations were executed in watercolor and pen and ink.
The text was set in 17-point Garamond.

www.houghtonmifflinbooks.com

Printed in the U.S.A.

Library of Congress Cataloging-in-Publication Data
Christelow, Eileen. Not until Christmas, Walter! / Eileen Christelow.
p. cm.
Summary: Walter, the family dog with a nose for trouble, creates problems for his young mistress because he keeps sniffing out and unwrapping the Christmas presents.
ISBN 0-395-82273-4 PA ISBN 0-618-24618-5
[1. Christmas—Fiction. 2. Dogs—Fiction.] I. Title.
PZ7.C4523No 1997 [E]—dc21 96-52217
CIP AC

WOZ 10 9 8 7 6 5 4 3 2

★ Contents ★

★ 1 ★
A Present for Walter

There were only two days until Christmas. Louise was making presents. She made a painting with yellow glitter stars for her dad. She made macaroni earrings with red glitter dots for her mom. She made a paper bag puppet with blue glitter eyes for her little brother, Harry.

"Don't worry, Walter," Louise said to her dog. "I'm going to give you a present too!"

RIGATONI
MACARONI
LOVE XXOO LOUISE

Louise walked down the hill to Bob's Grocery with Walter and Harry.

Walter had to stay outside while Louise bought an extra-large dog bone biscuit.

"Walter will *love* that present," said Harry.

Walter wanted his present right away. He sniffed and snuffled at the bag. He wheedled and whined.

"Not until Christmas, Walter!" said Louise.

When they got home, Louise wrapped the presents. Harry and Walter tried to peek.

"Go away!" said Louise. "You can't see—not until Christmas!"

Louise put the packages in the living room for everyone to see.

Walter sniffed and snuffled each package.

"Walter, they aren't *all* for you!" said Louise.

"He seems to think they all smell good," said her mom. "What are they?"

"You'll find out," said Louise. "But not until Christmas!"

That night, before Louise fell asleep, she told Walter, "Tomorrow we'll look for a Christmas tree in the woods. The next day is Christmas. Then you can have your present."

Walter wagged his tail. *Thump. Thump.*

But the next morning . . .
THE PRESENTS WERE GONE!

There were scraps of wrapping paper all over the floor.

"Who unwrapped the presents?" cried Louise.

"Not me!" said Louise's mom.

"Not me!" said Louise's dad.

"Maybe it was a robber!" said Harry.

"The robber left lots of clues," said Louise's mom.
"Sparkles on the rug!" said Harry.
"Chewed wrapping paper!" said Louise's dad.
"Sparkles on Walter's nose!" said Louise.

Walter wagged his tail.
His nose glittered and gleamed.
His ears glittered and gleamed.
"WALTER!" shouted Louise.
But Walter was slinking away

. . . to his bed in the kitchen, where they found:
a slightly chewed painting with yellow glitter stars,
crunched-up macaroni earrings with red glitter dots,
a slobbery paper bag puppet with blue glitter eyes . . .
and a little piece of extra-large dog bone biscuit.

"Walter, you are the robber!" cried Louise.

Walter sighed.

★ 2 ★

Walter in the Doghouse

Louise was so mad, she sent Walter out to his doghouse.

"Bad dog!" she shouted. "You won't get another Christmas present from me!"

Walter sighed again.

"Walter must have smelled dog biscuit on all of the presents," said Louise's mom.

"Walter has a stupid nose," grumbled Louise.

"You can't be mad all day," said Louise's dad. "Let's go look for a Christmas tree."

"Walter can't come," said Louise.

"Poor Walter!" said Louise's mom. "He can't stay in the doghouse all day."

"Woof!" said Walter. He followed them into the woods.

"Dumb dog!" grumbled Louise.

"What a scraggly bunch of trees!" said Louise's dad. "I don't see any good Christmas trees."

"Dumb trees!" grumbled Louise.

Louise walked from tree to tree.

"Dumb. Dumb. Dumb," she muttered.

Pretty soon she was humming,
"Dum–te–dum–
dum–tiddly–dum."

"Hey!" shouted Louise.
"We could tie two trees together!"
No one answered.

"Where are you?" shouted Louise.

Still no one answered.

Louise tried to follow her footprints backwards. But they zigged to the left and zagged to the right, around and around and around.

"I'm lost," whispered Louise.

Two tears rolled down her cheeks.

Then she heard a noise.

Sniff, sniff, sniff . . . snuffle, snuffle . . .

WOOF!

"Walter!" gasped Louise. "Am I glad to see you!"
"Walter found you with his nose!" shouted Harry.
"Good doggy!" said Louise. "What a smart nose!"

That evening Louise, her mom and dad, and Harry decorated their Christmas tree.

"Two scraggly trees tied together sure make one nice Christmas tree," said Louise's dad.

"Louise had a good idea," said Harry.

Before she went to bed, Louise put three new packages under the tree: one for her mom, one for her dad, and one for Harry.

Then she wrapped another extra-large dog bone biscuit for Walter.

"Walter's nose will never guess what is in this package," said Louise.

★ 3 ★
Walter Meets a Man Wearing Red

Before she got into bed, Louise tied one end of a string to Walter's package. She strung the other end all the way to her bed and tied two bells to it.

"Don't try to open your present," she told Walter. "Not until Christmas!"

Walter wagged his tail. *Thump. Thump.* They both fell asleep.

Several hours later, Walter woke up. He had been dreaming about a tasty, crunchy, extra-large dog bone biscuit.

Sniff, sniff, snuffle, snuffle.
Walter sniffed all the way down the stairs

. . . into the living room.

He sniffed and he snuffled all around the big box. He was just about to tear a tiny piece of wrapping paper off when he heard a noise in the fireplace . . . *Scritch, scritch scratch.*

WOOOSH!
WHUMP!

"Yeowlp!" yelped Walter.

He scrambled behind the couch.
He shivered and quivered.
Then he peeked out and saw . . .

. . . a roly-poly little man with a long white beard. He was dressed completely in red!

The hair stood up on Walter's back.

"G-r-r-r!" he growled. "GR-R-R-R-R!"

"Nice doggy," whispered the man in red.

He pulled a large dog bone biscuit out of his pocket.

As he handed it to Walter, he stumbled against the big box.

Jingle! Jingle! Jingle!
rang the bells on Louise's bed.
"Walter?" mumbled Louise.
"WALTER! Where are you?"

Louise quickly crept downstairs
and peeked into the living room.
"Walter!" she gasped.
"You opened your present again!"

But Walter had not opened his present.

"So, where did you get *that* biscuit?" asked Louise.

"Woomf!" said Walter.